Dear Parents and Educators,

Welcome to Penguin Young Readers! As parents and educators, you know that each child develops at his or her own pace—in terms of speech, critical thinking, and, of course, reading. Penguin Young Readers recognizes this fact. As a result, each Penguin Young Readers book is assigned a traditional easy-to-read level (1–4) as well as a Guided Reading Level (A–P). Both of these systems will help you choose the right book for your child. Please refer to the back of each book for specific leveling information. Penguin Young Readers features esteemed authors and illustrators, stories about favorite characters, fascinating nonfiction, and more!

Ice Cream Soup

LEVEL 1

GUIDED READING LEVEL **D**

This book is perfect for an **Emergent Reader** who:
• can read in a left-to-right and top-to-bottom progression;
• can recognize some beginning and ending letter sounds;
• can use picture clues to help tell the story; and
• can understand the basic plot and sequence of simple stories.

Here are some **activities** you can do during and after reading this book:
• Picture Clues: Sometimes, pictures can tell you something about the story that is not told in words. Have the child go through the book, and by just looking at the pictures, identify what toppings are placed on the ice cream cake.
• Make Connections: Have you ever helped someone make something fun in the kitchen? What was it, and how did you help?

Remember, sharing the love of reading with a child is the best gift you can give!

—Bonnie Bader, EdM
  Penguin Young Readers program

*Penguin Young Readers are leveled by independent reviewers applying the standards developed by Irene Fountas and Gay Su Pinnell in *Matching Books to Readers: Using Leveled Books in Guided Reading*, Heinemann, 1999.

For Karen G, who is sweet as a double dip
with sprinkles on top—AI

For Lily—RW

Penguin Young Readers
Published by the Penguin Group
Penguin Group (USA) Inc., 375 Hudson Street, New York, New York 10014, USA
Penguin Group (Canada), 90 Eglinton Avenue East, Suite 700, Toronto, Ontario M4P 2Y3, Canada
(a division of Pearson Penguin Canada Inc.)
Penguin Books Ltd, 80 Strand, London WC2R 0RL, England
Penguin Ireland, 25 St Stephen's Green, Dublin 2, Ireland (a division of Penguin Books Ltd)
Penguin Group (Australia), 707 Collins Street, Melbourne, Victoria 3008, Australia
(a division of Pearson Australia Group Pty Ltd)
Penguin Books India Pvt Ltd, 11 Community Centre, Panchsheel Park, New Delhi—110 017, India
Penguin Group (NZ), 67 Apollo Drive, Rosedale, Auckland 0632, New Zealand
(a division of Pearson New Zealand Ltd)
Penguin Books (South Africa), Rosebank Office Park, 181 Jan Smuts Avenue,
Parktown North 2193, South Africa
Penguin China, B7 Jiaming Center, 27 East Third Ring Road North,
Chaoyang District, Beijing 100020, China

Penguin Books Ltd, Registered Offices: 80 Strand, London WC2R 0RL, England

Text copyright © 2013 by Ann Ingalls. Illustrations copyright © 2013 by Penguin Group (USA) Inc.
All rights reserved. Published by Penguin Young Readers, an imprint of Penguin Group (USA) Inc.,
345 Hudson Street, New York, New York 10014. Manufactured in China.

Library of Congress Cataloging-in-Publication Data is available.

ISBN 978-0-448-46265-3 (pbk)   10 9 8 7 6 5 4 3 2 1
ISBN 978-0-448-46571-5 (hc)   10 9 8 7 6 5 4 3 2 1

Ice Cream Soup

by Ann Ingalls
illustrated by Richard Watson

Penguin Young Readers
An Imprint of Penguin Group (USA) Inc.

Look at me.

Look at what I can make.

I can make an ice cream cake.

I know what to do.

I have a plan.

First, I need a big blue pan.

I get a spoon.

I scoop some up.

One scoop, two scoops,

drip and drop.

Three scoops, four scoops.

Plop, plop, plop.

Five more scoops.

I think I can.

Six more scoops.

I fill the pan.

13

I pat it down.

I pat and pat.

Now I can add some of that.

Red and blue and yellow
and green.

This is the best ice cream cake
I have seen.

I pat it down.

I pat and pat.

Now I can add some of that.

Red and blue, big and small,

I think I have room

to add them all.

There is still room.

Yes, there is room for more.

I look for something

that I can pour.

I pour some here.

I pour some there.

I pour and pour everywhere.

There is more room.

I don't want to stop.

I can put something else

on top.

23

Look at my cake.

Look at it now.

I want to add more,

and I know just how.

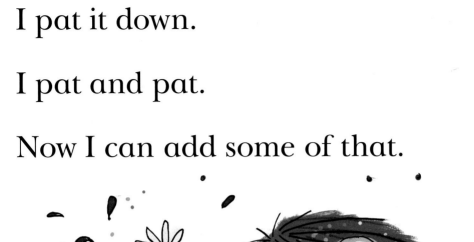

I pat it down.

I pat and pat.

Now I can add some of that.

Splat!

27

This is not cake.

This is a mess.

What did I make?

It looks like goop.

I think I made some

ice cream soup.

31

Yum!

E   Ingalls, Ann.

              Ice cream soup.

5/13

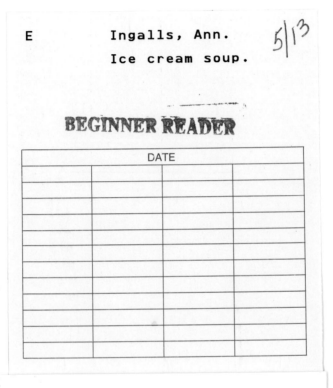

BEGINNER READER

DATE		